RIP VAN WINKLE'S RETURN

Adapted and Retold by **Eric A. Kimmel**
From **"Rip Van Winkle"** by **Washington Irving**
Pictures by **Leonard Everett Fisher**

Farrar, Straus and Giroux • New York

Long, long ago, before our country became a nation, a little Dutch village stood on the banks of the Hudson River, nestled against the foot of the Kaatskill mountains. The village had been there as far back as anyone could remember. The bricks in the walls of the oldest houses had come across the sea in sailing ships when the whole Hudson Valley was a colony of Holland.

Living in one of those houses—which looked as if it had not seen a nail or a coat of paint since the day in 1626 when Pieter Minuit bought Manhattan Island from the Indians—was a good-natured fellow named Rip Van Winkle.

The crumbling house was Rip's home, but no one in the village would ever seek him there.

"Rip Van Winkle? Look for him and his dog down by the riverbank. He's probably gone fishing."

The village children knew where to find Rip. He was their greatest friend.

"Rip, help us make a kite!"

"Rip, play marbles with us!"

"Show us that cave in the mountains!"

"Tell us one of your ghost stories!"

Rip Van Winkle always had time for children. Why wouldn't he? He never tended his own farm. His fences tumbled down and weeds grew in his field. What's more, his son and daughter went about as wild as if they had been raised in the forest by wolves. None of it troubled Rip. He took the world easy, preferring to starve for a penny than work for a pound.

Dame Van Winkle, his wife, was another matter. She was not content to whistle her life away.

"What is to become of us, Rip?" she would scream. "The house is falling on our heads. When are you going to mend the roof? A fox has raided the henhouse. The cow has gotten into the garden and eaten the cabbages. I cannot see the corn for the weeds. The children are crying because they are hungry. What am I to tell them? That we will eat when their father comes home from fishing? Fishing! With all that needs to be done, how can you waste time going fishing! It would not be so bad if you caught anything, but you never do. You sit on the bank watching the world go by, while your home falls to pieces."

Then Rip would smile and take her hand, softly saying, "Now, now, my dear. It is not as bad as that. I do catch fish, and rabbits, too, when I go hunting. A perfect husband I may not be, but we have always gotten by."

"Gotten by? Starving? Living in a ruin? That may be enough for you, Rip Van Winkle, but it will never be enough for me! My life has been cursed since the day I married you!"

Too angry for words, Dame Van Winkle would seize the nearest broom. Then Rip and his dog, Wolf, for their own preservation, would quickly take themselves off to the village inn.

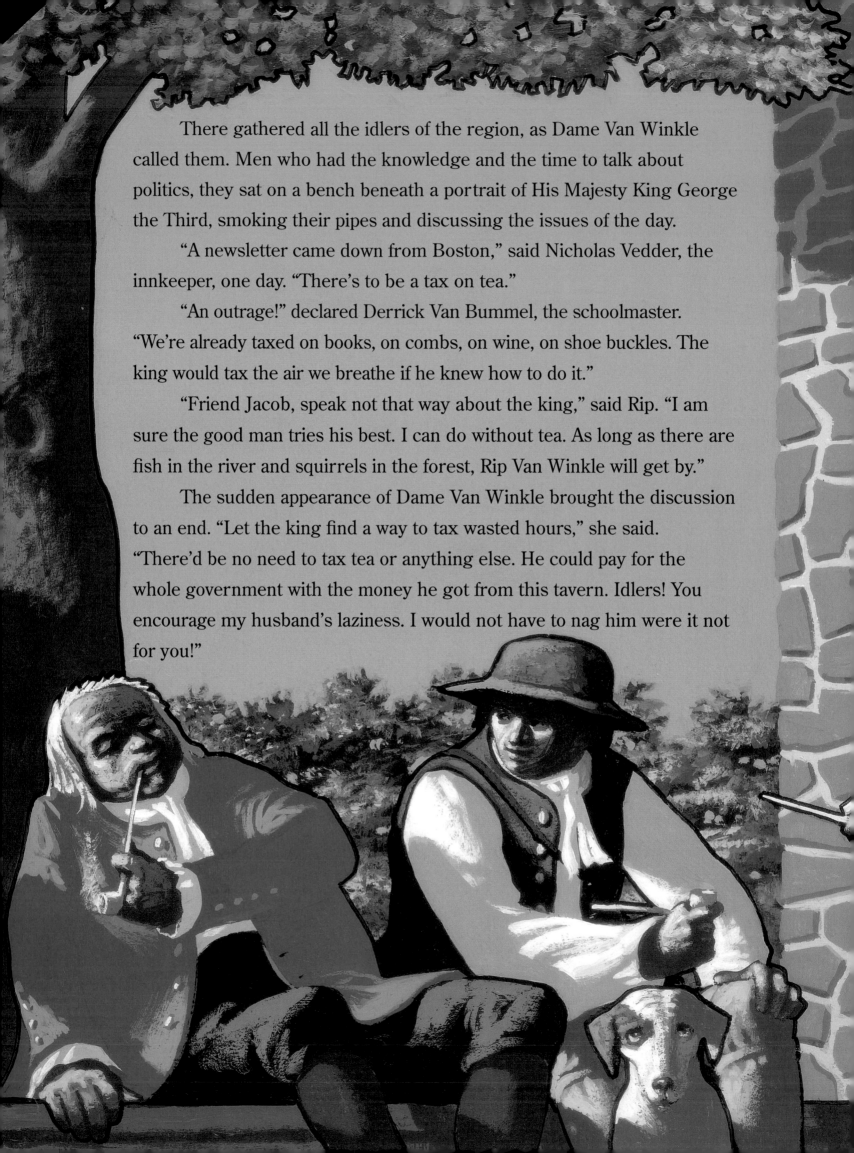

There gathered all the idlers of the region, as Dame Van Winkle called them. Men who had the knowledge and the time to talk about politics, they sat on a bench beneath a portrait of His Majesty King George the Third, smoking their pipes and discussing the issues of the day.

"A newsletter came down from Boston," said Nicholas Vedder, the innkeeper, one day. "There's to be a tax on tea."

"An outrage!" declared Derrick Van Bummel, the schoolmaster. "We're already taxed on books, on combs, on wine, on shoe buckles. The king would tax the air we breathe if he knew how to do it."

"Friend Jacob, speak not that way about the king," said Rip. "I am sure the good man tries his best. I can do without tea. As long as there are fish in the river and squirrels in the forest, Rip Van Winkle will get by."

The sudden appearance of Dame Van Winkle brought the discussion to an end. "Let the king find a way to tax wasted hours," she said. "There'd be no need to tax tea or anything else. He could pay for the whole government with the money he got from this tavern. Idlers! You encourage my husband's laziness. I would not have to nag him were it not for you!"

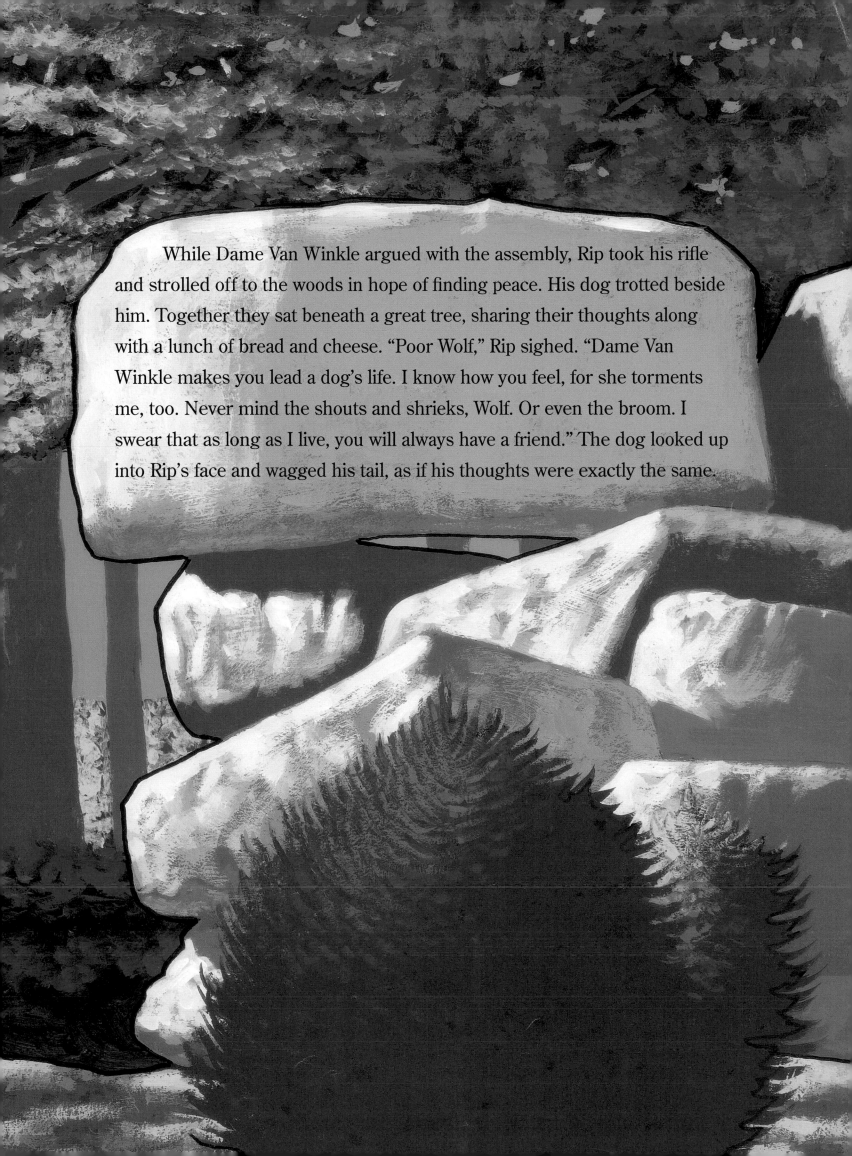

While Dame Van Winkle argued with the assembly, Rip took his rifle and strolled off to the woods in hope of finding peace. His dog trotted beside him. Together they sat beneath a great tree, sharing their thoughts along with a lunch of bread and cheese. "Poor Wolf," Rip sighed. "Dame Van Winkle makes you lead a dog's life. I know how you feel, for she torments me, too. Never mind the shouts and shrieks, Wolf. Or even the broom. I swear that as long as I live, you will always have a friend." The dog looked up into Rip's face and wagged his tail, as if his thoughts were exactly the same.

Rip continued until he and Wolf reached the highest part of the Kaatskills. He stopped to rest on a green knoll. Below, he could see the Hudson River moving on its majestic course. Rip sat there until it was time to return home. He shivered at the thought of encountering Dame Van Winkle.

Then, out of nowhere, he heard his name. "Rip Van Winkle! Rip Van Winkle!" Rip looked around. The only living creature in sight was a distant crow flying across the mountain.

Wolf growled. His hackles bristled.

Rip looked down into a darkening glen. He saw a figure climbing up the rocks, bent under the weight of a load on his back. As the stranger approached, Rip grew even more surprised, for coming toward him was an old fellow dressed in an antique Dutch fashion. On one shoulder he carried a keg, which appeared to hold some kind of liquor.

The stranger beckoned for Rip to help him with the load. Taking turns, they carried the keg up the dry bed of a mountain stream. Long, rolling sounds like distant thunder rumbled from a cleft in the rocks, as if a storm were passing over the mountains.

Rip followed his companion into the ravine. On the other side they came to a hollow surrounded by steep cliffs. There Rip saw a company of similarly clothed fellows rolling balls at nine wooden pins set up on the green. They reminded Rip of the figures in a Flemish painting in the town hall. It had been brought over from Holland more than a century ago, when the village was first settled.

No one spoke. Nothing broke the stillness but the sound of wooden balls rolling across the green. It echoed through the mountains like peals of thunder.

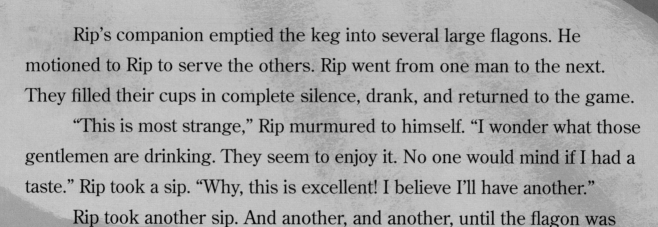

Rip's companion emptied the keg into several large flagons. He motioned to Rip to serve the others. Rip went from one man to the next. They filled their cups in complete silence, drank, and returned to the game.

"This is most strange," Rip murmured to himself. "I wonder what those gentlemen are drinking. They seem to enjoy it. No one would mind if I had a taste." Rip took a sip. "Why, this is excellent! I believe I'll have another."

Rip took another sip. And another, and another, until the flagon was empty. His eyes closed. He dropped to the ground. The flagon rolled on the grass as he sank into a deep and dreamless slumber.

Rip opened his eyes. He squinted in the morning sunlight. "Where am I?" he asked himself. "I'm back on the knoll where I first saw that fellow with the keg!" Then he remembered the hidden glen, the silent company on the green, and their game of nine-pins. And the flagon. "Oh, that flagon! That wicked flagon! I should not have drunk so much. I have slept here all night. What will I tell Dame Van Winkle?"

He looked around. His well-oiled rifle was gone. In its place he found a rusty old flintlock with a worm-eaten stock. "Wolf! Wolf, where are you?" He whistled for his dog, but Wolf, too, had disappeared.

"I'd best go home," Rip said. His joints ached. "Sleeping on the ground does not agree with me. How I long for my own bed, my own hearth, and a plate of Dame Van Winkle's molasses cookies, warm from the oven."

As Rip approached the village, he encountered a number of people. They were strangers, which puzzled Rip, for he thought he knew everyone in the region. Their clothes were of an unfamiliar style as well, which made Rip wonder if he had somehow wandered into a foreign land. Yet they all appeared to speak his language. "Hello, old man!" one said, stroking his chin. Rip stroked his own. To his surprise, he found he had grown a beard nearly a foot long!

Children and dogs crowded around as Rip entered the village. The children pointed and laughed. The dogs growled when Rip tried to pet them. Nothing seemed the same. Even the houses looked different.

"Where am I?" Rip asked himself. "Could I have taken a wrong turn and lost my way? No, this has to be my village. I am sure of it. The mountains still stand in their places. The river still flows the way it always has. Oh, why did I drink from that flagon last night? It has addled my head badly. I'd best go home. Dame Van Winkle will be angry, but I know she will make sense out of everything."

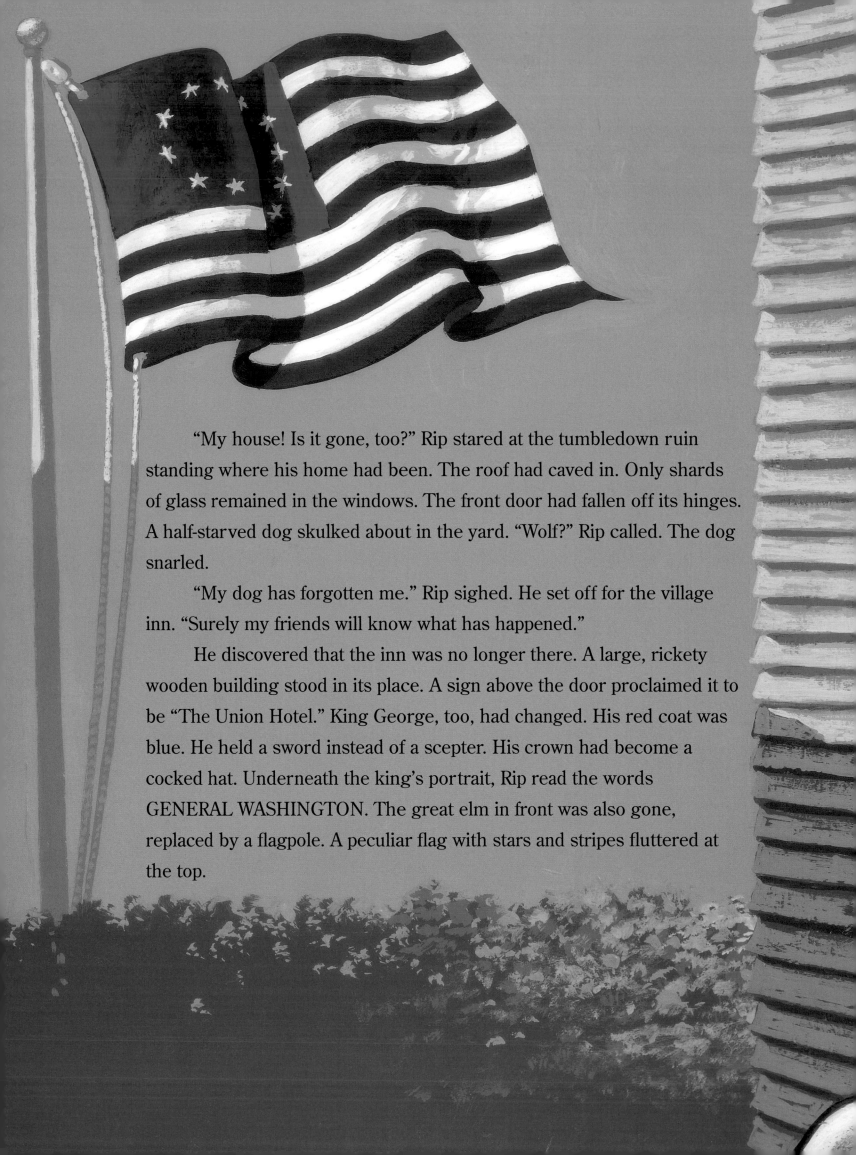

"My house! Is it gone, too?" Rip stared at the tumbledown ruin standing where his home had been. The roof had caved in. Only shards of glass remained in the windows. The front door had fallen off its hinges. A half-starved dog skulked about in the yard. "Wolf?" Rip called. The dog snarled.

"My dog has forgotten me." Rip sighed. He set off for the village inn. "Surely my friends will know what has happened."

He discovered that the inn was no longer there. A large, rickety wooden building stood in its place. A sign above the door proclaimed it to be "The Union Hotel." King George, too, had changed. His red coat was blue. He held a sword instead of a scepter. His crown had become a cocked hat. Underneath the king's portrait, Rip read the words GENERAL WASHINGTON. The great elm in front was also gone, replaced by a flagpole. A peculiar flag with stars and stripes fluttered at the top.

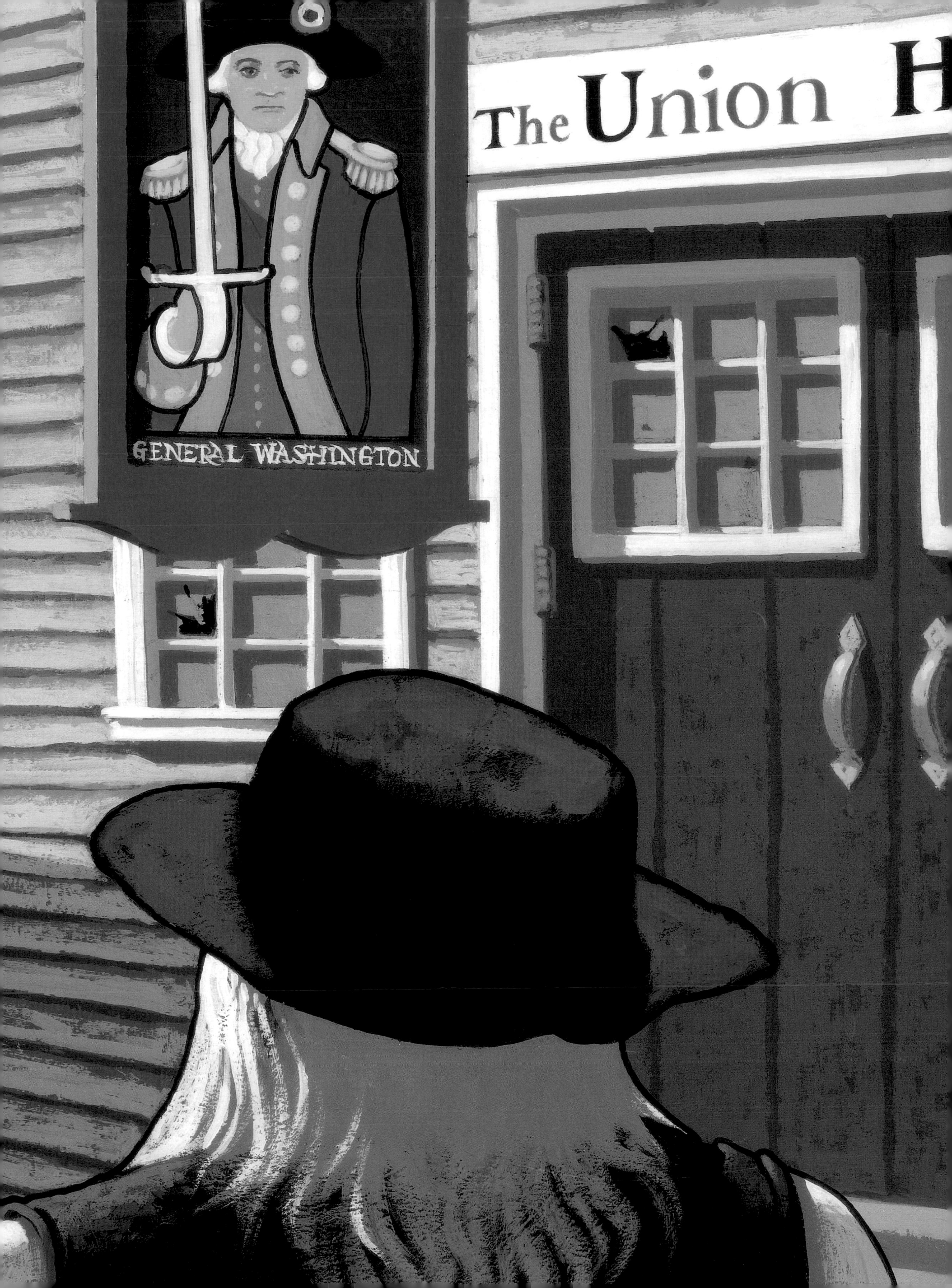
The Union H
GENERAL WASHINGTON

A crowd of people gathered to listen to a man giving a speech. He spoke of Bunker Hill, Valley Forge, liberty. None of it made sense to poor Rip Van Winkle.

He came closer to listen. The people in the crowd stared at him. The speaker pointed his way. "You, sir! What is your party? Are you a Federalist or a Democrat?"

Rip replied, "I am a loyal subject of King George, God bless him."

"A traitor! A Tory! Away with him!" someone shouted.

"I mean no harm," Rip said. "I only came looking for some of my neighbors who used to spend time here."

"What are their names?" a man in a cocked hat asked him.

"Nicholas Vedder, the innkeeper? He once owned this place."

"I knew him when I was a boy. He's been dead these eighteen years."

"Brom Dutcher?"

"Also dead. Killed at the battle of Stony Point."

"And Van Bummel, the schoolmaster? What of him?"

"He fought in the Revolution and became a general. You'll find him in Congress now."

Rip's world had vanished in a night. Everyone he ever knew was gone. "Does nobody here know Rip Van Winkle?" he asked.

"Certainly! Everyone in the village knows Rip. There he is, leaning against that tree."

Rip stared at the fellow. It was as if he were looking into a mirror, for the young man leaning against the tree was the very image of himself on the day he went up to the Kaatskills. "What has become of me?" Rip cried. "Someone has got into my shoes. I was myself last night when I fell asleep on the mountain. They took my rifle and now everything's changed. I'm changed. I can't tell my own name, or who I am!"

The bystanders nodded to one another. A few tapped their foreheads. This poor fellow had gone mad and needed to be locked up in a quiet place for his own good.

At that moment, a young woman came through the crowd, carrying a child in her arms. Something in her face awoke a memory in Rip. "What is your name, my good woman?" he asked.

"I am Judith Gardenier," she replied. "The man by the tree is my brother, Rip. He is named after our father, Rip Van Winkle, who disappeared in the Kaatskills twenty years ago. I was a little girl then, but I remember waving goodbye to him as he set off for the mountains. His dog, Wolf, came home the next day, but Father never returned. It was my mother's death. Despite her scolding, she loved our father dearly."

"I will pray that the poor woman found peace, for I gave her none," said Rip. He threw his arms wide to embrace his children. "Judith! Rip! I am your father! Young Rip Van Winkle once. Old Rip Van Winkle now. I beg your forgiveness, and that of your dear, departed mother. How right she was! Now I realize that I have been asleep. And not just for the years I slumbered in the mountains. I frittered my whole life away in idleness. No more! Come, Rip. You and I have work to do."

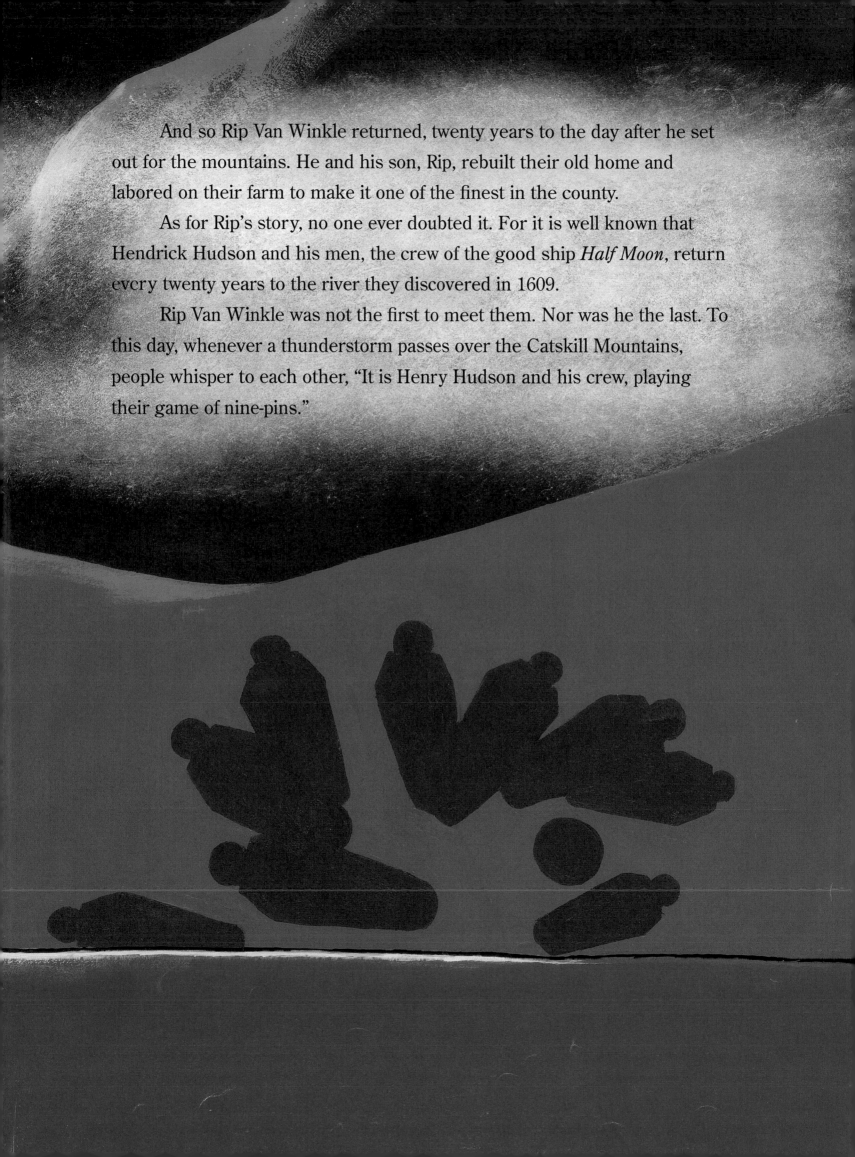

And so Rip Van Winkle returned, twenty years to the day after he set out for the mountains. He and his son, Rip, rebuilt their old home and labored on their farm to make it one of the finest in the county.

As for Rip's story, no one ever doubted it. For it is well known that Hendrick Hudson and his men, the crew of the good ship *Half Moon*, return every twenty years to the river they discovered in 1609.

Rip Van Winkle was not the first to meet them. Nor was he the last. To this day, whenever a thunderstorm passes over the Catskill Mountains, people whisper to each other, "It is Henry Hudson and his crew, playing their game of nine-pins."

Author's Note

Washington Irving (1783–1859) was one of the first American writers to become an international best-selling author. Two of his most famous stories, "Rip Van Winkle" and "The Legend of Sleepy Hollow," appeared in *The Sketch Book*, published in 1819. They have been classics of American literature ever since.

Irving spent many years living and traveling in Europe. From 1826 to 1829 he served as secretary of the American embassy in Spain. His fascination with medieval Spanish history and culture inspired several books, including *Alhambra*, a collection of stories from the Moorish kingdom of Granada, published in 1832. Ten years later, Irving's close friend Daniel Webster, the Secretary of State, arranged his appointment as U.S. Ambassador to Spain.

Irving died in Tarrytown, New York, located near the scene of so many of his stories. His home, Sunnyside, is now a museum visited every year by thousands of people from all over the world.

In adapting "Rip Van Winkle," I took the liberty of making two important changes. Irving presents Dame Van Winkle as a shrew without suggesting what might have made her that way. I saw her in a more sympathetic light. Being married to a ne'er-do-well who would rather hunt or fish or hang around the tavern than support his family would drive any woman to despair. I also gave Rip a chance to redeem himself. In Irving's story, Rip returns older, but not wiser.

To Dawn and Lowell

—E.A.K.

To Eric, colleague extraordinaire

—L.E.F.

Text copyright © 2007 by Shearwater Books
Illustrations copyright © 2007 by Leonard Everett Fisher
All rights reserved
Distributed in Canada by Douglas & McIntyre Ltd.
Color separations by Chroma Graphics PTE Ltd.
Printed and bound in China by South China Printing Co. Ltd.
Designed by Jay Colvin
First edition, 2007
1 3 5 7 9 10 8 6 4 2

www.fsgkidsbooks.com

Library of Congress Cataloging-in-Publication Data
Kimmel, Eric A.
    Rip Van Winkle's return / adapted and retold by Eric A. Kimmel from Rip Van Winkle
by Washington Irving; pictures by Leonard Everett Fisher.— 1st ed.
        p. cm.
    Summary: A man who sleeps for twenty years in the Catskill Mountains wakes to a
much-changed world.
    ISBN-13: 978-0-374-36308-6
    ISBN-10: 0-374-36308-0
    [1. Catskill Mountains region (N.Y.)—Fiction. 2. New York (State)—Fiction.] I. Fisher,
Leonard Everett, ill. II. Irving, Washington, 1783–1859. Rip Van Winkle. III. Title.

PZ7.K5648 Rip 2007
[E]—dc 22

2005042922